THE LITTLEST ANGEL

THE LITTLEST ANGEL

BY CHARLES TAZEWELL

ILLUSTRATED BY PAUL MICICH

ideals children's books.
Nashville, Tennessee

ISBN-13: 978-0-8249-5575-5   (hardcover)
ISBN-13: 978-0-8249-5549-6   (paperback)

Published by Ideals Children's Books
An imprint of Ideals Publications
A Guideposts Company
Nashville, Tennessee
www.idealsbooks.com

Library of Congress Cataloging-in-Publication Data
Tazewell, Charles.
   The littlest angel / by Charles Tazewell ; illustrated by Paul Micich
      p. cm.
   Summary: An earth-sick little angel newly arrived in the celestial king-
dom finds his recent transition from boy to cherub a difficult one.

[1. Angels—Fiction. 2. Christmas—Fiction.] I. Micich, Paul, ill. II. Title.
PZ7.T219Li 1991   91-2442
[E]—dc20   CIP
                                                AC

Printed and bound in the USA

Worz_Sep11_8

THIS BOOK BELONGS TO

_____

FROM

_____

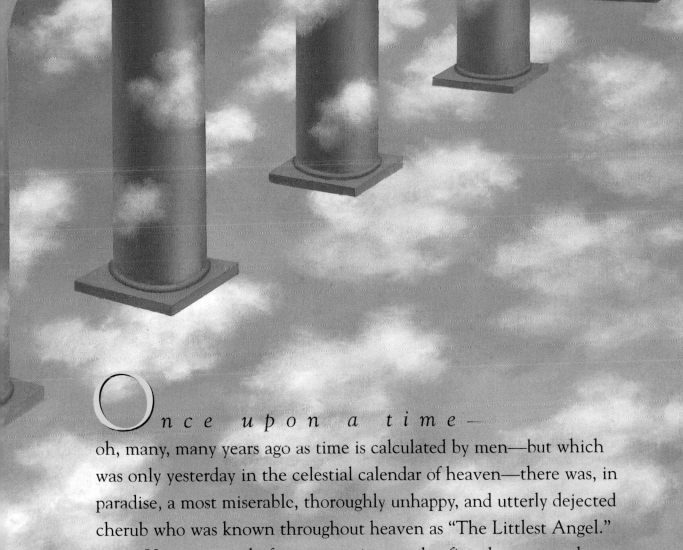

Once upon a time—
oh, many, many years ago as time is calculated by men—but which
was only yesterday in the celestial calendar of heaven—there was, in
paradise, a most miserable, thoroughly unhappy, and utterly dejected
cherub who was known throughout heaven as "The Littlest Angel."

He was exactly four years, six months, five days, seven hours,
and forty-two minutes of age when he presented himself to the
venerable Gatekeeper and waited for admittance to the glorious
kingdom of God.

Standing defiantly, the Littlest Angel tried to pretend that he wasn't at all impressed by such unearthly splendor, and that he wasn't at all afraid. But his lower lip trembled, and a tear disgraced him by making a new furrow down his already tear-streaked face—coming to a precipitous halt at the very tip of his small, freckled nose.

But that wasn't all. While the kindly Gatekeeper was entering the name in his great book, the Littlest Angel, having left home as usual without a handkerchief, endeavored to hide the telltale evidence by snuffing. A most unangelic sound which so unnerved the good Gatekeeper that he did something he had never done before in all eternity. He blotted the page!

From that moment on, the heavenly peace was never quite the same, and the Littlest Angel soon became the despair of all the heavenly host. His shrill, ear-splitting whistle resounded at all hours throughout the golden streets. It startled the patriarch prophets and disturbed their meditations. Yes, and on top of that, he inevitably sang off-key at the singing practice of the heavenly choir, spoiling its ethereal effect.

And, being so small that it seemed to take him just twice as long as anyone else to get to nightly prayers, the Littlest Angel always arrived late, and always knocked everyone's wings askew as he darted into his place.

Although these flaws in behavior might have been over-looked, the general appearance of the Littlest Angel was even more disreputable than his deportment. It was first whispered among the seraphim and cherubim, and then said aloud among the angels and archangels, that he didn't even look like an angel!

And they were all quite correct. He didn't. His halo was permanently tarnished where he held on to it with one hot, little, chubby hand when he ran, and he was always running. Furthermore, even when he stood very still, it never behaved as a halo should. It was always slipping down over his right eye . . .

Or over his left eye . . .

Or else, just for pure meanness, slipping off the back of his head and rolling away down some golden street just so he'd have to chase after it!

Yes, and it must be here recorded that his wings were neither useful nor ornamental. All paradise held its breath when the Littlest Angel perched himself like an unhappy fledgling sparrow on the very edge of a gilded cloud and prepared to take off. He would teeter this way—and that way—but after much coaxing and a few false starts, he would shut both of his eyes, hold his freckled nose, count up to three hundred and three, and then hurl himself slowly into space!

However, owing to the regrettable fact that he always forgot to move his wings, the Littlest Angel always fell head over halo!

It was also reported and never denied, that whenever he was nervous, which was most of the time, he bit his wing tips!

Now, anyone can easily understand why the Littlest Angel would, sooner or later, have to be disciplined. And so, on an eternal day of an eternal month in the year eternal, he was directed to present his small self before an angel of the peace.

The Littlest Angel combed his hair, dusted his wings, and scrambled into an almost clean garment, and then, with a heavy heart, trudged his way to the place of judgment.

He tried to postpone the dreaded ordeal by loitering along the Street of the Guardian Angels, pausing a few timeless moments to minutely inspect the long list of new arrivals, although all heaven knew that he couldn't read a word. And he idled more than several immortal moments to carefully examine a display of harps, although everyone in the celestial city knew that he couldn't play a note. But at length and at last he slowly approached a doorway which was surmounted by a pair of golden scales, signifying that heavenly justice was dispensed within. To the Littlest Angel's great surprise, he heard a merry voice singing!

The Littlest Angel removed his halo and breathed upon it heavily, then polished it upon his robe, a procedure which added nothing to his already untidy appearance, and then tiptoed in!

The singer, who was known as the Understanding Angel, looked down at the small culprit, and the Littlest Angel instantly tried to make himself invisible by the ingenious process of withdrawing his head into his robe, very much like a snapping turtle.

At that the singer laughed, a jolly heartwarming sound, and said, "Oh! So you're the one who's been making heaven so unheavenly! Come here, cherub, and tell me all about it!"

The Littlest Angel ventured a furtive look.

First one eye . . .

And then the other eye.

Suddenly, almost before he knew it, he was standing close to the Understanding Angel and was explaining how very difficult it was for a boy who suddenly finds himself transformed into an angel. Yes, and no matter what the archangels said, he'd only swung once. Well, twice. Oh, all right, then, he'd swung three times on the golden gates. But that was just for something to do!

That was the whole trouble. There wasn't anything for a small angel to do. And he was very homesick. Oh, not that paradise wasn't beautiful! But the earth was beautiful too! Wasn't it created by God, himself? Why, there were trees to climb, and brooks to fish, and caves to play at pirate chief, the swimming hole, and sun, and rain, and dark, and dawn, and thick brown dust, so soft and warm beneath your feet!

The Understanding Angel smiled, and in his eyes was a long-forgotten memory of another small boy from long ago. Then he asked the Littlest Angel what would make him most happy in paradise. The cherub thought for a moment and whispered in his ear.

"There's a box. I left it under my bed back home. If only I could have that?"

The Understanding Angel nodded his head. "You shall have it," he promised. And a fleet-winged heavenly messenger was instantly dispatched to bring the box to paradise.

And then, in all those timeless days that followed, everyone wondered at the great change in the Littlest Angel, for among all the cherubs in God's kingdom, he was the most happy. His conduct was above the slightest reproach. His appearance was all that the most fastidious could wish for. And on excursions to Elysian Fields, it could be said, and truly said, he flew like an angel!

Then it came to pass that Jesus, the Son of God, was to be born to Mary, in Bethlehem, in Judea. And as the glorious tidings spread throughout paradise, all the angels rejoiced and their voices were lifted to herald the miracle of miracles, the coming of the Christ child.

The angels and archangels, the seraphim and cherubim, the Gatekeeper, the Wingmaker, yes, and even the Halosmith put aside their usual tasks to prepare their gifts for the blessed infant. All but the Littlest Angel. He sat himself down on the topmost step of the golden stairs and anxiously waited for inspiration.

What could he give that would be most acceptable to the Son of God? At one time, he dreamed of composing a lyric hymn of adoration. But the Littlest Angel was woefully wanting in musical talent.

Then he grew tremendously excited over writing a prayer! A prayer that would live forever in the hearts of men, because it would be the first prayer ever to be heard by the Christ child. But the Littlest Angel was lamentably lacking in literate skill. "What, oh what, could a small angel give that would please the holy infant?"

The time of the miracle was very close at hand when the Littlest Angel at last decided on his gift. Then, on that day of days, he proudly brought it from its hiding place behind a cloud, and humbly, with downcast eyes, placed it before the throne of God. It was only a small, rough, unsightly box, but inside were all those wonderful things that even a child of God would treasure!

A small, rough, unsightly box, lying among all those other glorious gifts from all the angels of paradise! Gifts of such rare and radiant splendor and breathless beauty that heaven and all the universe were lighted by the mere reflection of their glory! And when the Littlest Angel saw this, he suddenly knew that his gift to God's child was irreverent, and he devoutly wished he might reclaim his shabby gift. It was ugly. It was worthless. If only he could hide it away from the sight of God before it was even noticed!

But it was too late! The hand of God moved slowly over all that bright array of shining gifts . . . then paused . . . then dropped . . . then came to rest on the lowly gift of the Littlest Angel!

The Littlest Angel trembled as the box was opened, and there, before the eyes of God and all his heavenly host, was what he offered to the Christ child.

And what was his gift to the blessed infant? Well, there was a butterfly with golden wings, captured one bright, summer day on the hills above Jerusalem and a sky-blue egg from a bird's nest in the olive tree that stood to shade his mother's kitchen door. Yes, and two white stones, found on a muddy river bank, where he and his friends had played like small, brown beavers, and, at the bottom of the box, a limp, tooth-marked leather strap, once worn as a collar by his mongrel dog, who had died as he had lived, in absolute love and infinite devotion.

The Littlest Angel wept hot, bitter tears, for now he knew that instead of honoring the Son of God, he had been most blasphemous.

Why had he ever thought that the box was so wonderful?

Why had he dreamed that such utterly useless things would be loved by the blessed infant?

In frantic terror, he turned to run and hide from the divine wrath of the Heavenly Father, but he stumbled and fell and, with a horrified wail and a clatter of halo, rolled in a ball of misery to the very foot of the heavenly throne!

There was an ominous and dreadful silence in the celestial city, a silence complete and undisturbed save for the heartbroken sobbing of the Littlest Angel.

Then, suddenly, the voice of God, like divine music, rose and swelled throughout paradise!

And the voice of God spoke, saying:

Of all the gifts of all the angels, I find that this small box pleases me most. Its contents are of the earth and of men, and my Son is born to be king of both. These are the things my Son, too, will know and love and cherish and then, regretfully, will leave behind him when his task is done. I accept this gift in the name of the child, Jesus, born of Mary this night in Bethlehem.

There was a breathless pause, and then the rough, unsightly box of the Littlest Angel began to glow with a bright, unearthly light; then the light became a lustrous flame, and the flame became a radiant brilliance that blinded the eyes of all the angels!

None but the Littlest Angel saw it rise from its place before the throne of God. And he, and only he, watched it arch away from heaven and shed its clear, white, beckoning light over a stable where a child was born.

There it shone on that night of miracles, and its light was reflected down the centuries deep in the heart of all mankind. Yet, earthly eyes, blinded, too, by its splendor, could never know that the lowly gift of the Littlest Angel was what all men would call forever,

"The shining star of Bethlehem!"